LEXIE
the Word Wrangler

Rebecca
Van
Slyke

illustrated by
Jessie
Hartland

NANCY PAULSEN BOOKS

exie was the best wrangler west of the Mississippi, and everyone knew it.

She wore a tall hat, fancy boots, and a bandana.

Like all wranglers,
Lexie could ride
a horse,

twirl
a lariat,

and herd cantankerous cattle where she wanted them to go.

But Lexie wasn't an ordinary wrangler.
Lexie was a word wrangler.

Lexie could tie words together.

She could take an ear of corn

and a loaf of bread

and make
some tasty

cornbread

She could take
a stick of butter

and a pesky
fly

BZZZZZ

and make
a beautiful

butterfly

In the spring, Lexie watched over the baby letters
on the ranch until they grew into bigger and bigger words.

cattle
cat
at
a

CATTLE

sagebrush
sage
age
a

sagebrush

Every morning in the chuck wagon,
Lexie mixed up a fresh batch of words.

She could
take an
annoying
P-E-S-T
and turn it
into some fine
P-E-T-S.

She could take
a small
S-P-O-T
and
make it
into
a

P-O-S-T.

Lexie could herd words into sentences.

For Sale:
BARN
Kittens

If y'all have a PEST problem, they will help you.
They also make great PETS!

Lexie
305-24...

Lexie
305-15...

Lexie
305-...

Lexie
305-24...

LEXIE
305-24...

Lexie
305-24...

She could hitch sentences together so they could do a job.

LEXIE

Dear Ma,
Life on the ranch is as fine as frog's hair. I'm busy putting in some POSTs for a new fence in a SPOT near the barn...

In the evenings, she penned
words together to tell a story.

Once upon
a time
there
were

three
little
jacka-
lopes...

Everyone agreed that
Lexie was a champion
word wrangler.

Nearly everyone, that is.

Lexie noticed that not all was well on the ranch.

At first it was little things.

When Lexie got dressed in the morning, she noticed that the d was missing from her bandana.

"Wranglers don't wear bananas around their necks," she said.

Then it was bigger things.

After a rainstorm, she looked up in the sky
and said, "Some varmint has stolen
the rain from the rainbow."

It was true.
Instead of a rainbow,
there was a bow
in the sky.

When Lexie rounded up a herd of calves
for a neighboring rancher, someone released
a whole passel of baby g's into the calf pen.
All the little dogies became doggies.

"I got me a bone to pick with some rascal," she said.

That night, when Lexie unrolled her sleeping bag, the twinkling S-T-A-R in the sky

turned into

R·A·T·S

"Ain't no fun sleeping out under the rats," she said. "Looks like we got us a word rustler."

Lexie dusted off her bedroll.

"I aim to find that word rustler and bring him to justice,"
she said, and she headed into the bunkhouse to sleep.

The next morning, she rode off into the desert to look for the word rustler.

to the dessert

But that rascal had added an S, turning the whole desert into a giant dessert.

"Don't that just take the cake,"
she said as she picked icing
out of her horse's hooves.

"It's high time to
trap this scoundrel,"
Lexie said.
She set a loop
in her lariat
and climbed a tree
by the barn to wait
for the word rustler
to strike again.

Lexie waited.

And waited.

Finally, along about sundown, Lexie noticed a shadow slinking along the corral where the longhorn cattle were. He was just about to steal the long from the longhorns when . . .

Lexie's
LONGHORN
Ranch

Lexie's rope snaked out!

"Looks like I caught me
a word rustler," Lexie said.
"What were you planning
to do, kid?"

"Aw, shucks. I wasn't
going to hurt the critters,"
the kid said.
"I was just aimin'
to have a little fun."

"And leave me
with a corral
full of horns?"
said Lexie.

"Darn tootin'," said the kid.

Lexie tried to hide a smile.
"What's your name, kid?"

"M-my name's Russell," he said.
"Please don't tell my pa."

"Justice must be done,"
said Lexie.

"Aw, shucks,"
said Russell.
"All I've ever wanted
was to work with words,
like you."

"You do seem to
have a talent for it,"
Lexie admitted.

Lexie's
LONGHORN
Ranch

She looked at Russell. "I hate to see good talent go to waste. If'n you can promise me you'll use your talents for good, maybe I can help."

"You've got my word," said Russell.

Lexie uncoiled her rope
from around the word rustler.
She lassoed up a big W and a little e . . .

Soon, Russell was no longer the word rustler.
He became Russell, the Word Wrestler.

Now Russell works side by side with Lexie on the ranch.

He helps her break
the wild words
in the herd.

He can take
a dangerous
rattlesnake
and

turn it
into a baby's
rattle

and a harmless snake.

He helps Lexie train the baby letters
to work together.

in
win
wing
swing

tree + house

treehouse

And Russell even helps the other young'uns learn to hitch words together . . .

. . . so they can become word wranglers themselves someday.

Dictionary of Wrangler Words

Here are some of Lexie's favorite wrangler words and their meanings:

Bandana—a square of cloth tied around a wrangler's neck, used to protect them from breathing the dust on the trail

Bedroll—blankets or a sleeping bag

Break—tame or train

Cantankerous—bad-tempered, ornery

Chuck wagon—covered wagon used for cooking

Corral—fenced area to keep animals in

Critter—animal

Dogies—orphaned baby cows, pronounced *doe-gees*

Herd—(1) a group of critters (2) to move a group of critters from one place to another

Jackalope—an imaginary critter made up of a jackrabbit and an antelope

Lariat—rope with a loop, designed to catch cows or horses

Lasso—to use a rope (lariat) to catch something

Longhorns—cattle with very long horns

Rascal/Scoundrel—someone who causes trouble

Rodeo—a show where wranglers show off their riding and roping skills

Rustler—thief

Varmint—pesky critter (or person)

Wrangler—cowboy or cowgirl

Thanks to Mike Casey at the Fairlea Longhorn Ranch
in Nicasio, California, for kindly giving me a tour.—J.H.

NANCY PAULSEN BOOKS
an imprint of Penguin Random House LLC
375 Hudson Street
New York, NY 10014

Text copyright © 2017 by Rebecca Van Slyke.
Illustrations copyright © 2017 by Jessie Hartland.

Library of Congress Cataloging-in-Publication Data
Names: Van Slyke, Rebecca, author. | Hartland, Jessie, illustrator.
Title: Lexie, the word wrangler / Rebecca Van Slyke ; illustrated by Jessie Hartland.
Description: New York, NY : Nancy Paulsen Books, [2017]
Summary: Lexie is a strong cowgirl who would rather wrangle words than cattle.
Identifiers: LCCN 2016003364 | ISBN 9780399169571
Subjects: | CYAC: Cowgirls—Fiction. | Vocabulary—Fiction.
Classification: LCC PZ7.1.V39 Le 2017 | DDC [E]—dc23
LC record available at https://lccn.loc.gov/2016003364

Manufactured in China by RR Donnelley Asia Printing Solutions Ltd.
ISBN 9780399169571
3 5 7 9 10 8 6 4

Design by Annie Ericsson.
Text set in Sentinel.
The art is painted in gouache.